New Bliss

MABEN HART
Published 2023

This work is released to

the public domain,

on purpose.

ISBN: 979-8-3747-2340-3

Dedicated to everyone who has ever had sex.

CONTENTS

Acknowledgments	i
Limericks	2
Sonnets	64
More	86
Index	106

ACKNOWLEDGMENTS

This book would have not come to fruition without Sacred Pleasure, written by Raine Eisler, inspiring the spark that lit my fire. Also, the leadership of Gala Darling and the self-guided exercises of The School of Life Design helped me make this dream a reality.

Special thanks to Derek, Evan, Nick, Rozzell, Ev, Gabby, Meghan, and Kat for believing in me and all my glorious friends who continue to shape me into a better person.

LIMERICKS

Spiritual Therapy

The touch of your face on my back
After a lascivious snack
Connects me to Goddess
In ways no one taught us
And ways which are fun to unpack

Workplace Reform

He dethroned the supervisor
Grazed her thigh with his incisor
When she asked for more
He ate to the core
Now shifts are short, his Love tranquillized her

Vulnerable

Her dreams and her soul on a platter
What used to mean worlds, doesn't matter
She took on a chance
To get into in my pants
And risk that our hearts may soon shatter

Fantasma Orgasma

She longed for a holy spasm
Fingers caused an orgasm
Loud and fierce
With a veil to pierce
Drenched her in ectoplasm

Excitement

Your smile makes me want to sing
Deep feelings swell up like a spring
I Love you so
My boat you row
You're my captain, I am your king

Historical Research

The birth of Venus from a shell
Makes the heart and vulva swell
Thoughts of lust
About her bust
The Roman goddess rings my bell

Our Religion

With age, as our values align
Perhaps I'll build you up a shrine
Worship me first
And make our pipes burst
Believing only what we define

Mutual Aid

Let me let you in my head
With you I want to share my bread
Let's talk it through
With focus on you
And move the service into bed

Beautiful Dancer

With one hand along my bust line
You admired my lovely design
We started to dance
In the sheets, in a trance
Wildly did we intertwine

Play Me

Your fingers nicely along
My ribs, like the notes of a song
On a top forty station
My favorite relation
Your fingers can never do wrong

For the Love of Aunt Flo

Nothing is ever taboo
Whether it's liquid or goo
As the red river flows
She flexes her toes
In response to a ruby bisou

Moon Goddess

Mother natures' BBQ
Fragile as the morning dew
Between the thighs
Are bluer skies
Darkening bed sheets when we screw

New Era Builders

With a voice that was booming clamorous
And a style that's no less than glamorous
They took my hand
And laid out my land
We created a world that is amorous

Flower Power

A swoon of joy swept them away
When they asked a femme to play
She agreed
And felt the need
To masturbate with her bouquet

You Grew on Me

When it began, I felt stuck
And I quickly ran off in my truck
But now we can tell
That we did ourselves well
You became my stroke of good luck

Boy Toy

He is my favorite thing to do
When the sun's out by the slough
And days are long
He sings my song
And we make love in a canoe

Blessed Connection

In my life you remain a fixture
On my altar sits your picture
For a Love ritual
To become habitual
I lay you on thick in my magic mixture

Worth the Wait

Once I fucked up long ago
She told me that I had to go
But my Love persisted
My soul grew and twisted
And now she adores me nouveau

Witchy Ways

Making space for fate
Takes time, it's getting late
So, open your arms
And legs and charms
Manifest and masturbate

Spell of Now

Gazing in the antique mirror
Our reflections become clear
Spreading trust
And acts of lust
Letting us live without fear

Once Again

She was my Love once before
But fate had surprises in store
I was left in the dirt
After making her squirt
And now she's back asking for more

Pay Up

It's fair to make them pay the toll
If they irritate your hole
A thousand bucks
For sloppy fucks
Or cut them off from rock n' roll

Midnight Fairies

In a late-night game of hide-and-seek
I experienced nothing unique
Until lead by a sprite
We took off in flight
And embraced until we were both weak

Hex Breaking

Lips no mortal dared to kiss
Until one simply whispered this
"I am like you
And I see you, too"
And now they are entwined in bliss

Workday

Waking from my deepest slumber
Responsibilities encumber
My sense of play
For the rest of the day
Until I booty call your number

Communication Sensation

Our friends won't approve of this
With your beau at home, we're in bliss
But consenting adults
See no wrong and no faults
In true Love's forbidden first kiss

Benefactor

His tongue was tied, so she tried to uncross it
Once she jumped naked out of his closet
She wrote out a plan
With her sexual man
And they promptly made a bank deposit

Evolution Solution

Colleagues taunted because he had no mate
With pay, she pretended to be his hot date
Night after night
Until tensions wore tight
And they boned until dawn in a cool, renewed state

Never Too Old

The last bang in one's life is always the best
It gets better with age, with fervor and zest
Until the last drip
Of love juice will slip
Into the abyss of the last snuggle fest

Hippie

She told me that she Loved me truly
Offered me assistance, coolly
Took off my pants
While in a trance
And made my home smell of patchouli

The Way of Wilde

The clothes you wear are always art
Of a libertine, you play the part
A classic vision
Of romance, risen
Bathed in sweetness, be the tart

Sometimes Third

Divine Lover, unicorn
Forever in you, Love is sworn
You're a go-getter
Who brings us together
Our hope for the future is born

Juice in Control

I long for the taste of your nectar
Of my film, you are the director
For only this week
So, make it good, speak
And tell me you'll be my protector

Mod Pod

I Love you in my social bubble
Your body has the softest stubble
Pussy cat whiskers
And magic elixirs
Help me explore and stay out of trouble

Cabaret Cuddles

Fishnets upon my shoulder
Making me feel a bit older
Like a man in a suit
With purpose, en route
Fingers up the thigh while I hold her

Bath Time Bestie

Allow me to your dreams uncloak
In my bathtub, please have a soak
We will play nice
With bubbles and ice
And shotgun top shelf weed we smoke

Too Busy

Eerie morning fog and dew
Reminds me of your morning goo
Sweet and sticky
So, leaving is tricky
When all I want to do is you

Book Club Sweetheart

Darling, precious bibliophile
When your bean stands erectile
My heart beats shake me
Your spell, you can take me
For books I walk the extra mile

Knowing One's Place

Feeling lucky to bone you
I'll never act like I own you
Every ounce is a treat
From your head to your feet
The world would be lucky to clone you

Write Again

A generous Lover is a generous friend
Dedicated until the end
In different ways
From nights to days
A poet with Love letters to send

Fantasy Penis

I want to do something more tactile
I wish my dick was prehensile
To lift up all things
And jump through small rings
Before becoming erectile

Natural Attraction

Her clit is like a firefly
It flickers when his mom goes by
Warm and alerting
When she is flirting
Her panties are no longer dry

Foggy Logic

Their friendship is full of good cheer
Together, rise above the fear
Of making mistakes
And long heartbreaks
For now lay low and hold them near

Good Riddance

There was an old man of great lust
Who favored the dames with a bust
From his bar, he was banned
So, he looked at his hand
As the only dame he could trust

Alternate Life

Finally forming a safer pod
At the risk of seeming odd
Loving, touching
Without clutching
Onto fear or a façade

Public Transit

All that is me and you and us
Whispering secrets in the back of the bus
Discretely reach
Into my peach
Quietly, without a fuss

Effigy Dildo

Infatuation with a man
Like an Oscar with a plan
Inside a flower
Half an hour
Reaching a galactic span

Young Love

A pile of blankets on the ground
To soften the excited pound
Of new libidos
Shooing mosquitos
With wild limbs flailing around

Royal Youth

Today, I feel like a queen
Who'll forever be nineteen
Sitting on face
Sent into space
With a rush of dopamine

Meshing Delicious

We're like jelly and peanut butter
You make my heart go all aflutter
When we mix
And do our tricks
In sacred spaces, free from clutter

Forest Frolic

Two young Lovers share a rose
And each other's favorite clothes
Flaunting goods
In magic woods
And humping where the red fern grows

Growth and Symbiosis

Oscillating to and fro
Really get the juice to flow
Both give and receive
Make Love believe
We still have a long ways to go

Strength in High Heels

Exhibiting such soft control
Slowly coming down the pole
I paid her fairly
And touched her, barely
In the club, my heart, she stole

Tease

Last night she sighed when I kissed her
Then I blushed when she called me 'mister'
My lips got wrapped in
From her nose to her chin
In a titillating, time traveling tongue twister

Be Loud

When magic from within does grow
And heavy feelings are in tow
Feel good loudly
Own it proudly
Be the star of your sex show

Snake Sex

Those serpentine movements you make
Cause the earth within me to quake
Watch how I dither
As your body does slither
Together we moan and we shake

Octopus

Limbs intertwined keep us warm
Behold, a glorious form
A big ball of glowing
With all tinges flowing
Love like a grand thunderstorm

Chill

With my best Love I feel great
Each moment is more like a date
Than a meeting of two
With nothing to do
Entwined, in an ambient state

Goddess

The strongest state of the femme
Who often hears the words "Je t'aime"
Can bat her eyes
To unzip flies
When she wants to shag, por tem

Procreation

When we want to get it on
We Loved each other until dawn
Sometimes we mate
With an open gate
And we create another spawn

Fecund

Relax with me and talk awhile
We can spend the day in style
Lounging nude
While we exude
The qualities of being fertile

Kinky Boot Strap

Because I was told I cannot
I've gained everything that I've got
With dazzling wits
And fabulous tits
And masturbating on pot

Intervention

The fingers of a thousand gods
Would put your pussy at great odds
With divine lust
An ancient thrust
And deep massages for your quads

The Sport of Acting

I think it would be very keen
If we acted out a whole scene
Of doing it all
On the floor and the wall
And everywhere in between

Mystery Terrain

The reigns of your chariot are in my hands
Guiding you towards my enchanted lands
Rivers of bliss
In a foggy abyss
Welcoming the warmth of moss and quick sands

Round Two

Two former Lovers took a chance
Rising in Love at second glance
Confessed their needs
And former deeds
And danced the cosmic bedroom dance

Wise Magic

You're a magician, too wise for cheap tricks
I'll tell you "I Love you" and hope that it sticks
If you tell me your secret
I'll forever keep it
And we'll cast our spells with a bodily mix

Hotness

Cleansing fires of passion
Are all the latest fashion
Light up hearts
And sensitive parts
Welcoming the crash in

Pulp

I supplicate your mango's squish
It's the most delicious dish
Sticky sweet
Familiar treat
It's everything that I could wish

Alpha

World blurring, handsome fool
Charming everyone at school
Lick the Mrs.
Pricks and kisses
Excite every molecule

Run For It

Run with passion through my fields
With seeds ready to give great yields
You find my G spot
In a parking lot
On a few different windshields

Accommodations

It's too hot, so stay over there
While we both put up our hair
And spread our thighs
To the moon in the skies
And show from afar how much we care

New Buzz

Butterfly kiss while wearing a mask
Podding up protocol, well worth the ask
Makes indoors more fun
Like a vigorous run
Drunk off connection straight from a flask

Remedy for Sleeplessness

Tired, in missionary position
The moment will come to fruition
To blast off into sleep
No need to count sheep
Rely on this old superstition

Time Out

It's necessary to take
At least a quick pee break
If you go long enough
When the going gets tough
And endless pleasure's at stake

Take Five

When stresses at work are abreast
And patience is put to the test
Take a moment to come
And you won't feel glum
Time it, for a personal best

Self-Sufficiency

The toy I keep in my pocket
Gets me there like a rocket
Fits cozy and snug
Like Love in my rug
Or like a knob in a socket

Bedside Manners

Request, whimper and moan
That is the order and tone
Communicate clearly
With the one you hold dearly
And always turn off the phone

Leveling Up

When aiming to match a vibration
One must focus on the creation
Combining the soul
To make a new whole
And practice with much masturbation

Little Black Book

Each page with a number addressed
Retracing your steps, ask who's best?
The one you've known always
Unnoticed in hallways
Yet separate from the rest

The Old Story

Echos of heartbreak knock at the door
When needs go unmet and we search for more
Sex without meaning
Leaves us all dreaming
With Love as a cheap game for which to keep score

Pretend We're at the Library

Quiet coming is better than none
When alone, in the mood for some fun
Or with a good friend
With sex needs to tend
Two whispers are better than one

Judge Me

I seek out an honest critique
Of my patented topping technique
But you may have to wait
While I open the gate
And let out my innermost freak

Worth It

Paying for labor is sexy as hell
Like bright neon colors in a world of pastel
Transferring cash
After having a splash
Ensures future visits will likely go well

Getting Through College

A loyal mistress deserves the best
Give her riches, and let her rest
Support her plans
And Only Fans
And then invite her to your nest

Boner Unwelcome

Drunkenly he tried to clobber
Into bed to touch and slobber
She pushed him off
Without a scoff
Of her peace he could not rob her

Be Sure

Stoking the flame of a date
Into a potential mate
May feel like a hex
If it does delay sex
But good things are well worth the wait

Waiting for Spring

Spending the entire day
Lounging in our lingerie
Makes my clit harden
Like tilling my garden
With extra time for foreplay

The Gift of You

Grateful to be up your thigh
Your boundaries I gladly comply
Your open fig
Its juices I swig
When you text, I'll swiftly reply

Another Time

Dear sweet infatuation
I feel like I'm on vacation
When I see you
But I can see through
My own toxic expectation

Sugar You

I Love you with each drop of my sweat
Max out my cards into debt
A Love language of money
Can make rainy days sunny
I'm giving without a regret

Mars and Venus

Touch me from my neck to my belly
Make me wet with natural jelly
Let's flop around
From the couch to the ground
Like a scene from a Botticelli

Twinks in Their Twenties

Let's wrestle in our pajamas
You have the cutest bandanas
You use them for flagging
With your pants slightly sagging
Let's snuggle and suck on bananas

A Poet's Obligation

Lost in a fog we hold tight
To when we knew we were right
Embracing the past
We know it won't last
We make Love and we come, and we write

Fix Your Pipes Gently

I am your perfect gentleman
I'll do everything that that I can
To ease your pain
Unclog your drain
And go down on you, to Chopin

Wild Lovers

For you I'd gladly break the law
You cause hearts to melt and ice to thaw
A desert rose
Where fortune grows
Let's make Love here, in the raw

Faded Starlet

You play a good scrabble game
Once wild, you are now quite tame
I feel the start
Open holes, open heart
Ignite feelings far better than fame

Stockings Sublime

Fingers along my black tights
Bring feelings of passionate nights
That silky texture
Drives me to text her
While I dim my bedroom lights

Sew In Love

I'll let you sleep late in my bed
So you can rest your sweet head
After a long night
Of being held tight
You're the needle to my thread

Quickies

"Friendly" is far from "obedient"
Your pizazz is my favorite ingredient
In every dish
You are my first wish
And I like how our romps are expedient

Rainbow Shorts

Comfy, cozy rainbow shorts
Cradle my ass into ports
My Love's at sea
The addressee
Of letters of the sultry sorts

Partnership

I Love you as much as my cat
It's been years, but I feel like that
A grown human being
I believe what I'm seeing
I'll pleasure you, tit for tat

Eve

For her touch, I have an affinity
She longs to be in my vicinity
Stronger than me
A natural queen bee
I crave the taste of her salinity

Out and About

Take a chance to light a spark
When you're flirting in a park
Make connections
Bask in reflections
Deepen sweetly in the dark

More Than Dating

Proper courtship slipping through
The fingers of the god in you
On a hot date
They'll gladly wait
As dreams are built upon the new

More to Love

I've loved you through my lowest ages
From deep inside my self-made cages
When I am under under
As we moan like thunder
Of my book of life, you're my favorite pages

Riverfront Sesh

Meet me at the waterfront
Maybe we can share a blunt
Practice flirts
With hands up shirts
Without putting up a front

Global Warming

It's too hot for us to screw
In our bed, nothing to do
So, take up space
At your own pace
And I'll do me, while you do you

Naked and Famous

She threw herself into a mission
For the perfect exhibition
She opened the doors
And pulled down her drawers
Intentions had come to fruition

Elderly Love

Flesh as the petals of flowers
Into the evening hours
In life's autumn season
Love outweighs all reason
With seasonal sexual powers

Bright Nature

The sunshine never gets old
On every skin cell that I hold
Warm me in the breeze
Make me weak in the knees
A hot kiss on my face when it's cold

Outdoor Bathtub

Cool porcelain on a hot day
Below a spring waterway
Two souls collide
In the vastness outside
Bringing chills straight up each vertebrae

My Skin is Bark

Twisting as branches of trees
Elbows around knobby knees
Shaking with splendor
And total surrender
Quivering leaves in a breeze

Melty

They came to me in a dream
I thought I was going to scream
They ignited a fire
With lust and desire
In my sweet bowl of peaches and cream

#9

Scratching the summertime itch
Fine tuning the art: to bewitch
Entice and adore
To worship and more
Make Love while eating the rich

Octopus Hug

The distinct palpation of suction
Instills a remembered conduction
Each tentacle thrill
Up my spine sends a chill
In a dance of aquatic seduction

Bugging Out

I have a strange question to ask
About an insectile task
My dear astral expositor
Be my ovipositor
And let my ambitions unmask

Cat Naps

First thing in the morning my fat kitty purrs
Warm in the sunshine, coziest furs
Between thick thighs
The heat mystifies
Through my work plans, we must take detours

On the Morning Commute

Finding myself in a pickle
Riding on my bicycle
I want to get off
Like a rebel's Molotov
And allow for my juices to trickle

Within the Community

Seeking pleasure, long nights are drifting
In and out, a veil lifting
To clearly see
In front of me
My desire cosmically shifting

SONNETS

New Era Orgy

Once we had thought we had given up hope
Now we Love life and look forward to more
Unravelling like the string of a rope
Limbs all wild and sprawled on the floor

Eager fingers lock strong hand in hand
Beckoning lips call upon others
A friendly milking of the prostate gland
And all the most alluring stepmothers

A feast for the eyes and all the senses
All the moments are rolled into one
A faint Pollock of somebody's menses
Decorates the altar of sacred fun

Overwhelmed with gratitude for my pod
Bringing out everyone's inner sex god

Natural Affair

Summoning me to the edge of the wood
Stood a womyn who was more of a fox
On the most magical trip to Mt Hood
I felt a magnet from her to my box

She looked over her shoulder right at me
And winked and smiled and waved me on over
She was the most beautiful sight to see
With mossy hair and clothing of clover

She took my hand, laid me down in the grass
With fingers from heaven, she grazed my skin
From above, reached under and grabbed my ass
She played my pussy like a mandolin

As we came, she faded into the mist
Leaving her clover wrapped around my wrist

Divination

Asking my tarot where to kiss you first
Leaving my fingers searching for yours
You scratch my itches, you quench my thirst
Patching my holes and unlatching my doors

Open my windows to let in the breeze
Open your legs and trust your own feelings
If you lightly yearn, I drop to my knees
Roofs become floors and floors become ceilings

Fiction bleeds truth as I taste you in me
Knowledge and blessings from my deck of cards
You are the smoke that flows through my chimney
Music that plays in my favorite backyards

Here I feel safe, like the year twenty ten
With my tarot deck, hot sex and a pen

Explosions Within

Shouts of passion echo through chamber halls
Bodies collide in ethereal mist
Pinned up against the sides of bedroom walls
Vines of pleasure sprout and grow as they twist

Around wrists with bliss as mouths move with grace
Over mountains and valleys with delight
I lick up your body, caress your face
Melt ourselves together into the night

Exploding colors behind eyes closed tight
Breath on breath in understood confusion
Peeling back sacred truths and feeling right
As though the world is just an illusion

Collecting the stars bursting in the air
Settling like sand on skin that's so bare

Lesbian Spring

When we both wear our favorite spring dresses
The world stops turning, with all eyes on us
Flawless makeup, ready to make messes
Stopping traffic from inside a bus

No matter who's ready and who is not
To see such beauty transcend gender norms
I feel so good when I know I look hot
Nothing about my trans body conforms

The bird of individuality
Has awoken and flown from its dark cage
Creating a new, queer, reality
Mating in public to get rid of the rage

Femme sex all over, at parks and bus stops
Bottoms who get enough Love become tops

Catlike Love

The Bastet of my life, your way, you paw
Into my ball of yarn, you like to play
Snagged deep into my beating heart, your claw
Hooks me like a hopeless fish on Sunday

Dance around me and shine your beauty out
So that you may absorb, reflect and such
You give me a feline, level-eyed pout
I'll do anything for you, soft to touch

The Love you send me forms great protection
My confidant, my idol, and my dear
Near you I always have an erection
Come closer, darling, and purr in my ear

Bed down on my pillow, what's mine is yours
Your Love for me opens the divine doors

Prioritizing Pleasure

Chaos ensues, no one pays attention
With flailing thoughts, and feelings, and limbs
Muscles relax as though easing tension
Is built into ritualistic whims

A little planning goes a long, long way
Setting sail onto a vast ocean
Like the never fading Dorian Gray
But rather than beauty lies devotion

A longing to nourish every desire
A Lover could possibly have inside
When the sun sets, we choose to retire
Prioritizing pleasure before pride

Life is sweeter with blissful parts planned out
With time to be silent and time to shout

Exhibitionist Debut

I want to ride you atop a mountain
So, the shouts of our Love echo throughout
The forest, as we turn on your fountain
I put my lips to your small pleasure spout

Tasting the nectar of sweet life itself
Melting into the mossy atmosphere
Knowing the wisdom of the woodland elf
Believe in forest magic over fear

Your juice gives me strength out there in the woods
Intertwining eternal life forces
What is mine is yours, please share my goods
Creating new magic from old sources

Atop a mountain, I want to ride you
And make our exhibitionist debut

How We Met

Her glorious smile, nothing could outshine
I saw her from far away and I knew
My life was changed that day on the coastline
Ever since then my affinity grew

For spooky, loud dames who know who they are
I told her that I liked her blue sweater
She said "Yeah, me too" and got in a car
And then stopped, and my panties got wetter

Then she asked me if I wanted a ride
She meant on her face, and I was in bliss
She slipped in her fat tongue way up inside
I'll never forget our very first kiss

Now she's my mate and I'll stay next to her
When everything else in life is a stir

Pulp of Life

A mouth missing a body can still speak
Truths about longing and passionate days
Lightly fingers on the softest nipples tweak
As thoughts run through my mind in wild ways

Out my fingertips into my own skin
Spelling out the future I desire
Feelings of a lover's body within
And plans of inner growth do conspire

Freckles map the skin as stars map the sky
Angels praise the tracing of such mapping
The pulp of life begins to electrify
The ritual of the great unwrapping

Intentions set bring souls together close
And moments grow, just like an acid dose

Galactic Features

Only deep breaths can tame my wild heart
It races when I think of you near me
It's the End, but also a perfect start
Something new, something real, divine, carefree

Warm hands are the best, I can feel them now
A metaphysical imprint that stays
We'll create a plan, but I don't know how
Perhaps we should pleasure, while we stargaze

Wanting each other more than we can stand
It's more complex than I had imagined
Orgasmic sensation that wants to expand
In ways unseen and spoken by the wind

Your alien ways speak to my new soul
When we kiss, we open up a wormhole

Pheromone Fire

You can wrap your snake around my aura
If you want to penetrate my fruiting
Lips you can; you're fauna to my flora
Excitedly our parts protruding

You can rub yours on mine any which way
It feels good for me, I come with such ease
Between all the feels I cherish our play
The hairiest nipples, I like to tease

I am your obsession, like it or not
You want me around every day, I know
Let's keep this fire of pheromones red hot
Only with boundaries and space can we grow

Secure attachment styles turn me on
So, meditate and evolve or be gone

Venusian

Vermillion lips pressed up against mine
Strong shoulders, thick waist, I was her captive
Threw me on the bed as pearls before swine
I'm not worthy and she was attractive

I let her take me in her swollen arms
With pleasure I didn't know existed
Vulnerably, I leaned into her charms
Nothing of her could be resisted

Her mouth caressed me, I passed into hips
And melted into the depths of her night
She gripped my thighs with painted finger tips
I was lost in the darkness, she was bright

I'll worship her silently all my days
She taught me to Love in classical ways

Get Topped

Kegels are sanctified, old magic tricks
The one thing we can do to grab ahold
Of power with power and get our kicks
Gazing into eyes with futures untold

Wielding the reigns of the carriage of lust
Go in whatever direction I choose
Feeling the courage to do what I must
Releasing sweetness summoned by my muse

After my release I'm still in control
Clenching my muscles so you don't forget
Higher on life than when smoking a bowl
Sending Morse codes of what you don't know yet

Relax and get topped, and let worries flow
Away in the night and let yourself grow

Sweet, Sticky Miracles

Ancient wisdom oozes from peach fuzz lips
As fingers dip deeply down to the pit
Sweet, sticky miracles gather in drips
To be licked up in an orgasmic fit

Truth found between her legs is a blessing
Baptize myself within the vulva dive
One may find their fingers gently pressing
Upon their pulse to see if they're alive

Sex mixed with Love is the greatest feeling
Conspiring eternal cosmic laws
Within a vacuum, one's mind is reeling
Like a wild feline sharpening her claws

Ready to run, to pounce into unknown
Places where the nature is overgrown

New Sexperience

Turn off the Lo-Fi and let the birds sing
Open the window, my dear darling friend
We put phones on silent, so they don't ring
We touch our feelings until the day's end

Little pink flaps of tender care and joy
Are sweeter than dessert on my tastebuds
Safely sharing my utmost favorite toy
We fling open the gates creating floods

Washing me clean of previous battles
Your nectar is life to my heart and soul
Please ride me like your favorite saddles
And let me meet this achievable goal

Let your Love make me glisten in the sun
Clean me up and we'll cuddle when we're done

Long Autumn Days

On long autumn days lonely fingers crawl
Up prickly skin to find fruits awaiting
Underneath a blue cloudless sky I sprawl
Between my thighs, energy creating

Timelines of when I was Loved intersect
I feel all of them twist into one now
Never have I felt so hot with respect
And I'm grateful for being here somehow

Angels evolve into still higher states
Shedding wings and living with us for play
Tasting sweet fruits and nuts from silver plates
And wearing the finest of lingerie

I think of them on my long autumn days
And pleasure mySelf while paving new ways

Into Later Years

Waiting for death as though Love never came
Won't change what was, what is, or what will be
Waiting for Love is an outcry of shame
Action wins hearts over complacency

Waiting for dating, creating, wanting
Becoming fixed in ways of solitude
Hiding away what you could be flaunting
Overcome the fear of coming off rude

Revel in the sweetness and pleasure and spice
Ask all of the questions; cats' out of the bag
The hardest step is to just break the ice
Whether ovulating or on the rag

Or whether the flower petals have died
Keep aiming to shag, so you know you tried

Hooky

Calling in sick and hiding out with you
Perhaps forever under warm covers
Kiss and a snuggle and another screw
Fallen space angels and human Lovers

Camping indoors in our homemade love nest
Use my arm as a pillow, cradling
Magic embodied in flesh, in your breast
With you I feel comfort in labeling

Love, trust, adventure and security
My cup overflows when you are around
We break down the myths of impurity
With head in the clouds and feet on the ground

Secret sabbatical from nine to five
Making me grateful to be alive

MORE

Serpentine

I am a dragon, come under my wing
Tell me of the riches you intend to bring
While we lay here, sky clad under stars
Tell me the stories tied to your scars
I'll lick each one with my fat dragon tongue
While you sing me promises that can only be sung

Coven Rituals

Vibrant nails scratch my itches
And caress me through the day
Matching with my other witches
When we want to play

Penetrating ripened fruit
Causing juice to squirt
We bond our bodies and transmute
The passions we assert

Then and Now

The ethereal touch of a Lover of past
Turns sunny days to overcast
Only the touch of a Lover that's new
Can release the soul, so the spell can undo

Bro Gaze

Dick pics don't compare
To the way you blankly stare
In my direction
At my erection
Without warning
In the morning
Stretching out my gray sweatpants
Is something near beyond bromance

Waking Up

Stepping into solar rays
Feeling every cell get warm
Planning to have better days
And be the calm within the storm

So let me get this fire started
Down below the belt
And dive into this place uncharted
To feel what I once felt

Commitment in the Age of War

When you are near, my pain, it goes
To where no one really knows
I feel fantastic in your arms
More than the work of basic charms
There is something deep in me
That craves to please you properly
Perhaps it's fate, or something more
Something we both are asking for

Little Death

Let the world melt away
And let each cell expand
Into a rainbow life bouquet
Of overflowing sand
Through an hourglass mirage
And with a steady pace
Like strong hands giving a massage
That shoot you into space

Art Party

Washable marker on prickly skin
In all the colors of youth
Kissed by the sunshine, Loved from within
Spelling out pictures of truth

Colorful bodies like trippy cartoons
With secrets written discreetly
Dance in their lust and their trust under moons
Shining down upon rainbows sweetly

Adventure

The better you can please yourself
The better a Lover can
Communicate to release yourself
Make an elaborate plan

Perhaps plan a treasure hunt
Although it may sound freaky
Roll up a big pleasure blunt
And make each other leaky

Community Building

An angel whispered in my ear
The truth is what they want to hear
The play and scoring of tired games
Will never win the hearts of dames

Ask what they want in a cosmic Lover
And listen to their reply
If it's not you, introduce your brother
And all who would give it a try

Virtual Affair

Although two Lovers are far away
Their screen brings them together
Exploring dimensions of sexual play
Never for worse but for better

If all intentions are ripe with consent
Nothing can go wrong
The future story of your own present
Will sound like a Love song

Living Art of Great Importance

You make up the pieces
Of my favorite collage
The words of my thesis
And Love's camouflage
Blending our ways
By silken moonlight
At the ends of our days
When all moments are right

Body Topography

Exploring over territory
Mindfully and slow
Every crevice tells a story
That I want to know

Fingers gliding create trust
Weaving a foundation
Talking thoroughly about lust
And every sensation

Once one body is explored
We begin the other
Both are worshiped and adored
As a trusted lover

Special Skills

We boned our way into a cloud
Very high, and equally proud
Overachievers
And newfound believers
Of the power we have when we're loud

Orgasm On a Bicycle

When the vibration hits
On a bike, just right
And the tips of your tits
Begin to pinch tight
Let it out, just go
Feel all the tingles
No one will know
As your bike bell jingles

Sex Toy

Tiny matchbox wheels
Up and over tickling lightly
From the button to the heels
Inspires smiling brightly

Skin becomes prickly with goosebumps
Driven from the path of the tires
Through valleys and over love lumps
Into mutually shared desires

Monster of Me

If I had a tail, it would wrap around you
If I had claws, they would scratch your back
I'm so glad that I have found you
For Loving me, you have a knack

If I had wings, I'd fly you to the moon
And I'd share the air from my lungs
Like the ephemeral form of a sand dune
Let our bodies twist like our tongues

Sleeping Feline

Don't wake up the kitten
She sleeps between your feet
I know that we are smitten
But keep your bedding neat

Don't wake up the cat
She's curled in a ball
So, try to come just where you're at
With me on top, and all

Backyard

Dare to let impassioned moans
Out into the breeze
Resonate angelic tones
When muscles start to seize

Let bodies shake with rapture
Be loud in open air
And realities will fracture
Elated fragments here and there

Pick up the pieces left behind
Settled in the grass
From licking lips and being kind
To sharing sacred ass

Progress

That was a little bit rough
And the grip was a little bit tough
But we talked about it
And will now do without it
Because we're creative enough

Everything at Once

Gently play the other parts
Instruments in a band
And reading astrological charts
Complexities at hand

Caress all over, checking in
"Do you like it this way?"
A crashing "YES" comes with a grin
In a rapturous buffet

Volcanoes of ecstasy begin to arise
Where there once were tits
Tongue like the warmth of a mountain sunrise
Caressing all the bits

Rule Book

Anxious to play
And anxious to fight
Makes sunny days
Darker than night
Tranquil to speak
And tranquil to be
Makes our knees weak
And our libidos free

Covid Era Commitments

Please put on my favorite mask
And dance my favorite steps
If you want it all, please ask
And squeeze my huge biceps
I'll do what it is you want
And say what you want to hear
If you request it, I can flaunt
Whatever keeps you near

Shag in the Street

Now is the time to shag in the street
And shag like never before
Connection never tasted so sweet
And never had so strong a pour

A choice to be made: the 'same old', or 'thrive'
Rome wasn't built in a day
Choosing right now to feel alive
And shag in the street in feeling gay

Sex Goddex

All the times we bone are sacred
Worthy of respect
There's ritual in getting naked
To be the architect
Build the frame of Love to make
A blueprint to explore
A vast adventure to undertake
Behind the bedroom door

Long Term Depth

Little flings are overrated
Depth is like a drug
Once a spell has resonated
Offer up a hug
Dig deep into a Lover's mind
To find their truest being
And break apart the daily grind
To begin feeling, seeing

Oasis

Lovers' lips to blow cool air
On a sultry day
Caressing hips up to the hair
And then invite to play

In the shade, we're going slow
Between the sun's bright rays
Tasting as the fruit hangs low
Each other's cherry glaze

Dystopian Fling

Mystery behind the mask
Two adults consent
Meeting for a sexy task
Leaving all content

Clothes fly off, on goes protection
Mask still covers face
Adding to Love collection
With a quick embrace

Dance of Life

To come every day
Is a healthy routine
Make time for play
Keep your pipes clean

To orgasm daily
Will keep your thoughts clear
So, roll around gaily
With whom you hold dear

Obsession Confession

I'll sew the belt loop of which I tore
When I pulled you near me
And rub your shoulders when they're sore
And always hold you dearly

I'll aim to come with you twice a day
As a solid routine
And take in every word that you say
And the silence in between

Fortress Seduction

Build me a fort like it's spring 2020
When you moved into my house and called me honey
Let's kiss under sheets propped up by chairs
Tell all our truths and fulfill our dares
Inside is safer; you're all I need
Until we branch out and all become freed

Spell of YES

One more juicy, salty word
Drips from the lips awaiting
Let out the sweetest sounds I've heard:
The call of human mating

"Yes", the sound, it opens gates
Of gushing softness futuristic
"Yes" share this spell with lucky mates
And then experience something mystic

For Lovers Only

The warmth of human breath does hold
The wonders of the earth
We want to feel loved when we're old
Beginning with self-worth

The very special someone to breathe on
Will come excitedly to you
Like a pup with a toy to teethe on
Getting lost in the chaos of new

Return of the Octopus

Tentacles, they pull me closer
Emerging from behind
Her back, she gave a second dose, her
Feelers read my mind

Licking holes that don't lick back
And then some that do
Rest your head on the sweet rack
Of the cosmos when you're through

Home Movies

The sun is out, the coast is clear
Roommates are away
Dress up in lace and hold me near
Together we press 'play'

Images of you and me
Frame by frame in motion
A wholly natural sight to see
Basking in devotion

Thick wet lips meet thick wet lips
Pressing upon arrival
And thick sharp hips meet thick sharp hips
An animalistic revival

Skin to skin transfers a power
Fully present in this
On the screen, a precious flower
Blossoms with a kiss

INDEX

#9, 60

A Poet's Obligation, 49
Accommodations, 38
Adventure, 91
Alpha, 37
Alternate Life, 25
Another Time, 47
Art Party, 90

Backyard, 96
Bath Time Bestie, 20
Be Loud, 30
Be Sure, 46
Beautiful Dancer, 7
Bedside Manners, 41
Benefactor, 16
Blessed Connection, 11
Body Topography, 93
Book Club Sweetheart, 21
Boner Unwelcome, 45
Boy Toy, 10
Bright Nature, 58
Bro Gaze, 84
Bugging Out, 61

Cabaret Cuddles, 20
Catlike Love, 70
Cat Naps, 61
Chill, 31
Commitment in the Age of War, 85
Communication Sensation, 15
Community Building, 91
Coven Rituals, 83
Covid Era Commitments, 98

Dance of Life, 101
Divination, 67
Dystopian Fling, 100

Effigy Dildo, 26
Elderly Love, 57
Eve, 54
Everything at Once, 97
Evolution Solution, 16
Excitement, 5
Exhibitionist's Debut, 72
Explosions Within, 68

Faded Starlet, 51
Fantasma Orgasma, 4
Fantasy Penis, 23
Fecund, 33
Fix Your Pipes Gently, 50
Flower Power, 9
Foggy Logic, 24
For Lovers Only, 103
For the Love of Aunt Flo, 8
Forest Frolic, 28
Fortress Seduction, 102

Galactic Features, 75
Get Topped, 78
Getting Through College, 45
Global Warming, 56
Goddess, 32
Good Riddance, 24
Growth and Symbiosis, 28

Hex Breaking, 14

Hippie, 17
Historical Research, 5
Hooky, 83
Home Movies, 104
Hotness, 36
How We Met, 73

Intervention, 34
Into Later Years, 82

Judge Me, 44
Juice in Control, 19

Kinky Boot Strap, 33
Knowing One's Place, 22

Lesbian Spring, 69
Leveling Up, 42
Little Black Book, 42
Little Death, 90
Living Art of Great Importance, 92
Long Autumn Days, 81
Long Term Depth, 99

Mars and Venus, 48
Melty, 59
Meshing Delicious, 27
Midnight Fairies, 14
Mod Pod, 19
Monster of Me, 95
Moon Goddess, 8
More Than Dating, 55
More to Love, 55
Mutual Aid, 6
My Skin is Bark, 59

Mystery Train, 35

Naked and Famous, 57
Natural Affair, 66
Natural Attraction, 23
Never Too Old, 17
New Buzz, 39
New Era Builders, 9
New Era Orgy, 65
New Sexperience, 80

Oasis, 100
Obsession Confession, 101
Octopus, 31
Octopus Hug, 60
On the Morning Commute, 62
Once Again, 13
Orgasm on a Bicycle, 94
Our Religion, 6
Out and About, 54
Outdoor Bathtub, 58

Partnership, 53
Pay Up, 13
Pheromone Fire, 76
Play Me, 7
Pretend We're at the Library, 43
Prioritizing Pleasure, 71
Procreation, 32
Progress, 96
Public Transit, 25
Pulp, 37
Pulp of Life, 74

Quickies, 52

Rainbow Shorts, 53
Remedy for Sleeplessness, 39
Return of the Octopus, 103
Riverfront Sesh, 56
Round Two, 35
Royal Youth, 27
Rule Book, 97
Run For It, 38

Self-Sufficiency, 41
Serpentine, 83
Sew In Love, 52
Sex Goddex, 99
Sex Toy, 94
Shag in the Street, 98
Sleeping Feline, 95
Snake Sex, 30
Sometimes Third, 18
Special Skills, 93
Spell of Now, 12
Spell of Yes, 102
Spiritual Therapy, 3
Strength in High Heels, 29
Sugar You, 48
Stockings Sublime, 51
Sweet, Sticky Miracles, 79

Take Five, 40
Tease, 29
The Gift of You, 47
The Old Story, 43
The Sport of Acting, 34
The Way of Wilde, 18
Then and Now, 84

Time Out, 40
Too Busy, 21
Twinks in Their Twenties, 49

Venusian, 77
Virtual Affair, 92
Vulnerable, 4

Waiting for Spring, 46
Waking Up, 85
Wild Lovers, 50
Wise Magic, 36
Witchy Ways, 12
Within the Community, 62
Workplace Reform, 3
Worth It, 44
Worth the Wait, 11
Workday, 15
Write Again, 22

You Grew on Me, 10
Young Love, 26

ABOUT THE AUTHOR

Maben Hart thrives in the Pacific Northwest, spending the days mending hearts and holes, and the nights exploring astral realms. They grew up in Florida, but they breathe with the mountains. Maben likes to play music, dance, plan life by numbers, propagate plants, raise warm living things, and get into the sun as much as possible. Adult diagnosed autistic, they are a survivor of sexual assault and domestic violence, and have an unwavering optimism towards the power of Love as a healing art.